MOLLY BANG

TIGER'S

FALL

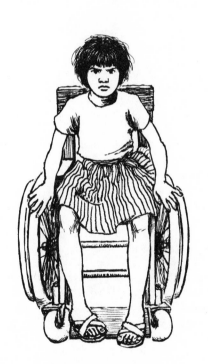

HENRY HOLT AND COMPANY · NEW YORK

*To the memory of Vania, whose radiance and quiet deter-
mination affected everyone who met her; with thanks to
everyone at PROJIMO who helped me with this story,
including Antonio, Armando, Conchita, Elena, Enrique,
Gabriel, Julio, Manolo, Mari, Miguel, Polo, Raymundo;
and with thanks and love, of course, to Trude and David.*

Henry Holt and Company, LLC
Publishers since 1866
115 West 18th Street, New York, New York 10011

Henry Holt is a registered trademark of Henry Holt and Company, LLC

Library of Congress Cataloging-in-Publication Data
Bang, Molly. Tiger's Fall / Molly Bang.
p.   cm.
Summary: After eleven-year-old Lupe is partially paralyzed in an accident in
her Mexican village, other handicapped people help her realize that her life
can still have purpose.
[1. Physically handicapped—Fiction. 2. Accidents—Fiction. 3. Self-perception—
Fiction. 4. Depression, Mental—Fiction. 5. Mexico—Fiction.] I. Title.
PZ7.B2217 Ti 2001   [Fic]—dc21   2001024567

ISBN 0-8050-6689-6 / First Edition—2001
Printed in the United States of America on acid-free paper. ∞

1   3   5   7   9   10   8   6   4   2

TIGER'S FALL

CHAPTER ONE

Lupe jumped the black stallion over the two other plastic horses, landed him neatly in his red velvet box, and hid the box way under the bed. One more thing Angelica was not going to play with or even see.

Lupe hadn't seen her cousin since last year, when they had all been at the home of other relatives, but then she had been a snob and a complete pill. Now Angelica's parents were going someplace on business and couldn't take her along. This was going to be a rotten week. At least it was November, and they'd be in school most of the time.

Out on the veranda, Lupe's younger brother Luís sat looking at the roof to see if the lizard might come out. It lived under some of the tiles that had come loose in the rains, and every few days when they heard it move, it sounded bigger.

HONK! HONNNNNK!

The bus squawked from the far edge of the village, announcing its arrival.

"Luís! Lupe! Now!"

Their mother quickly lifted baby Flor from the mat where he lay sleeping and tied him on to her back with her shawl.

They hurried down the main street of smooth, hard dirt and turned onto a rocky narrower side street, then another, stepping carefully over the ruts and stones as they heard the bus rumble closer: three streets away . . . two. . . . In front of a little grocery store they stopped and caught their breath.

Their mother turned to them. "Look at me, both of you," she said. "Now, you know Angelica doesn't understand our country life. I expect you two to help her and treat her kindly. Do you understand me?"

"Yes, Mama."

The bus heaved itself around the corner, braked to a halt, gave a long, exhausted sigh, and let its doors flap open.

Several people from the village got off. Señora Ruís held two baskets overflowing with little stuffed toys for her store. Señor García carried a pile of boxes with pictures of different faucets on them—he was probably doing plumbing on more of those rich villas in the hills. Then Angelica appeared on the top step, and Lupe's mouth almost dropped open.

How can she dress like that when she's only eleven, like me?

Angelica wore a bright yellow dress, dangling purple earrings, and purple lipstick. A pair of headphones was clasped to her head. She squinted here and there, as though expecting somebody other than the three familiar people who stood waiting in front of her. Finally she slid a pair of silver reflective sunglasses over her eyes, took a deep breath, gritted her teeth into a smile, and stepped politely into the arms of her Tía Estela.

The driver handed down an enormous gold plastic suitcase from the top of the bus. Luís and Lupe each grabbed hold of one strap and took a step forward. The suitcase hardly budged. They both lifted with both hands and lurched forward. Up ahead, Angelica was chattering to their mother, completely ignoring them as she described her family's new house in Mazatlán.

"I have my very own bedroom with all new furniture, white with gold trim, and a fluffy white rug, and my bathroom has its very own Jacuzzi, too. The movie room downstairs has these soft comfortable seats even better than the ones in a theater."

She babbled on and on. And on.

Estela made listening noises for a while, then said, "Angelica, what do you remember about our village from the last time you were here? It was four years ago, I think."

Angelica looked around. "Ooooh, I remember these yellow and pink and green houses," she said. "They look just like cakes all coated with colored icing. Your house is blue, isn't it? I remember 'cause we got a fountain in our new backyard. It's painted all blue inside, and right away I thought of your house!"

As Angelica looked up at her aunt, smiling benignly as though she'd just bestowed her with jewels, the smooth soles of her shoes slipped on a rock. She stumbled a few steps off the side of the road, her foot landing on a small brown toad, which until that moment had been successfully making itself invisible among the brown stones.

The toad leaped up in terror and found itself tangled in the yellow folds of Angelica's dress. As it tried to scramble up the cloth, Angelica screamed and batted at it. Flor woke up and started crying.

Lupe and Luís dropped the suitcase and ran over, yelling,

"Step on a toad and no rain for a year!"

"Step on a toad and no rain for a year!"

Angelica stopped screaming for a moment and stared at them in horror, then started screaming louder and batting more frantically while the poor toad hung on for dear life.

Estela reached over and pulled the skirt of Angelica's dress out flat. The toad dropped to the ground and crawled away to the wall.

Angelica broke into sobs. Estela put her arms around her while Lupe and Luís patted Flor, cooing and kissing him until everybody quieted down.

Angelica lifted her wet face from her aunt's protective bosom and glared at her two cousins in fury.

"What do I care about your stupid rain? I'll step on any toad I want! I'll squash it flat as a tortilla if I want, and it'll be dry as bones up here for ten whole years! Stupid, stupid superstition! Only children from a village would believe that anyway!"

Estela watched her children draw back, watched their faces flicker with shame, then anger, then close down as they stared at their miserable cousin. She felt Angelica

relax and then pull back as she realized what words had just poured out of her mouth.

"Come, let's look at something," Estela said. "All of us."

She walked a step to the wall and pointed to the round lump of the toad as it sat trying to look like a rock again.

"Stay back, so it doesn't get scared again," she said. "But look closely. See how its skin is all covered with little bumps, like warts? All toads have poison in their skin— enough to make them taste pretty nasty to any bird or small animal who wants to eat them. Many toads have enough poison to hurt people—if they pick them up.

"I think maybe a long time ago somebody was afraid their children would play with toads and hurt themselves, so they made up stories that would keep the children safe. For example, I know a child who just *loves* scary things. . . ." Estela looked over at Lupe, who kept her eyes intently on the toad. "And maybe only stories like those would keep that child from picking up a toad and bringing it back home.

"Most of the time there's some good reason behind a superstition," she said. "Poor old toad. I bet it's scared with these five giants staring down at it. Even Flor looks like a giant to a toad. Let's go home, my giant children, and get something to drink."

Luís looked over at his cousin. "You can see El Diablo, Angelica," he said. "He's our black stallion. Maybe we'll even let you ride him tonight. Sometimes he bites, but not usually."

CHAPTER TWO

That evening, when their father rode El Diablo back from the cornfields, the children took him out to the pasture where he could graze and rest with the mules and other horses from the village. When Angelica saw the stallion, she stayed far away from him and said her parents didn't allow her to ride except in the city. So in the evenings, Lupe rode El Diablo out to pasture alone, as usual.

She walked home when the sun had set but the sky was still light. The few people she passed were tired after a long day of labor and only nodded to her in greeting. The animals knew the day's work was done, so each quiet twitter and moo and whinny they uttered only added to the sense of peace in the hills and along the stream.

At the high end of the village Lupe waved to Señora Reyes, who was out in her courtyard cooking supper under her grapefruit tree. She called Lupe over and handed her three big grapefruit. "For you and your city cousin," she said, and smiled. "They're pink inside, and sweeter out here in the country."

Lupe thanked her and cradled the big yellow balls in her arms, taking big sniffs as she picked her way down the rocky alleyway. Lush green trees and a few black satellite dishes showed behind the darkening white walls. Lupe crossed through the park in the central square, opened the door, gave the grapefruit to her mother, and sat down with Angelica, Luís, and Flor to watch cartoons until supper-time.

After school during that long week, Angelica listened to her Walkman, wrote to friends back home, painted creative designs on her nails, and watched TV. Whenever she walked around the village with her cousins, she would remark on how "cute" the stores and houses were, how "sweet" and "old-fashioned" the church or the school was, and how much richer and cleaner and more exciting and more fun it was in the city.

But Angelica was finally leaving—tomorrow.

The three children sat around after lunch until Estela shooed them away. "Outside!" she ordered. "You're blessed with healthy bodies! Go use them! Run! Play! Go splash in the river! All three of you—now!"

The cousins plodded down toward the river, each one thinking how wonderful life would be when Angelica went home again. They looked out at the low hills, where the green bushes and grasses were turning brown but the flowering *ampa prieta* trees poked up unexpectedly in spots like bright reddish purple bouquets. Far beyond, hazy in the distance, rose the high Sierra Madres, the

"Mother Mountains." A single snow-covered peak floated above the rest.

Last year in school Lupe had learned that the long chain of mountains was made by plates of rock under the sea that pushed against the land all along the western coast of Mexico and far north into the United States. The plates squashed the land into higher and higher folds, but as wind blew and rain fell on the peaks they carried the dirt back down again, grain by grain, along the rivers and out to sea. Lupe kicked the dirt on the path as she walked, helping to speed it on its way.

As they rounded the last bend, they saw Señora Reyes coming up from the river with her laundry. Just ahead to their right was the ancient fig tree—a huge, luxuriant presence that reigned over the patch of land around it. The shadow of the tree fell across the trail. As Luís and Lupe greeted Señora Reyes, all three of them left the trail and walked around the shadow, making sure to stay in the sunlight.

Angelica stopped. "Why didn't you walk on the shadow?" she asked. Lupe and Luís just shrugged their shoulders.

"Oh, child," said Señora Reyes, "Catalina Perez drowned right here a few years ago in the flood waters. We don't step on the shadow—well, for her memory, you know? Some people do say her ghost sleeps up there in the branches, waiting for more companions to take away with her. But don't you believe that talk."

"Oh, I don't believe in superstitions," Angelica assured her. She turned and walked right onto the shadow and down the path.

As though a movie had switched on in her head, Lupe saw an image of Señora Perez coming through the door— years ago when their mother was sick. She had brought soup and a big bread stuffed with squash paste, and Lupe saw again her red skirt, heard her loud, fruity laugh, almost tasted the sweetness of that bread. She saw the faces of Señora Perez's sons at her funeral as the small boys stood beside the grave and stared at the white lacy cross. All around the cross lay bunches of plastic flowers in clear plastic wrapping that reflected pieces of the broiling sun.

Lupe couldn't bear to be around Angelica for another minute. Fuming, she marched quickly down the trail. Just as she reached the river, a cloud of yellow butterflies burst from the mud, floated around her head, then broke apart and zigzagged away in all directions. Lupe opened her arms to them and laughed out loud.

Behind her she heard Luís and Angelica talking about riding the bus. She climbed up onto the ledge of rocks and boulders, waved, and turned away as the two of them walked by and waded into the shallow milky water. Lupe moved slowly over the rock, exploring, looking for dark blue stones to take home.

Suddenly she stood still.

Big and fat and limp and loosely curved, almost as pale as the boulder it lay across, a rattlesnake warmed itself in the afternoon sun. Lupe backed off, silent as a shadow, her eyes searching, searching, finding. Slowly she stooped, picked up two rocks . . . a third . . . then crept back. She edged closer—still without a sound—stopped, lifted her arm, aiming, aiming, aiming . . . and threw.

The snake thrashed in the air, its tail reaching up, flailing, its rattle whirring in a frenzy. But the rock had smashed its head. In a few moments it lay still.

Lupe looked for Luís and Angelica. They had waded all the way over to the sandbar in the middle of the river and were just coming back—two dark silhouettes with sparkling water dancing all around them. They hadn't noticed a thing. Lupe pulled the snake off to the side of the rock where no one would see it and went to cool her feet in the river.

Just before supper, as soon as she had finished taking El Diablo out to pasture, Lupe ran back, picked up the dead snake, and let it fall in folds into her book bag. When she got home again, she lifted the covers of the bed she shared with Angelica, arranged the snake, covered it with the blanket, and joined the family for a special cup of goodbye cocoa and cookies before bed. Her father told funny stories about himself and Angelica's dad when they were little boys.

Lupe let Angelica get into bed first.

CHAPTER THREE

Angelica leaped out of the bed screeching like a demon. She screamed so hard, Lupe saw the tendons in her neck stand out like strings. Angelica's arms and legs jerked as she jumped around the cold cement floor in her bare feet and her long white nightgown with blue satin ribbons, hugging herself and screaming. The neighbors on both sides rushed over to see what had happened and stood with Lupe's parents at the door of the bedroom to stare.

Lupe tried to look sympathetic, but she could not hide her immense satisfaction—even after her parents grounded her for two weeks beginning the moment Angelica left.

Ah, tomorrow, tomorrow. At noon.

The next morning Lupe woke as she heard her parents getting out of their bed across the room. She heard them pulling on their clothes in the darkness, heard her mother

murmur to Flor as she lifted him and carried him out. Through the closed curtain she could see the veranda light go on, and soon she heard her mother grinding the corn for tortillas.

Lupe snuggled under the covers and listened to Angelica breathing beside her: regular, slow, quiet. From far away she could hear the faint fast throb of the motor pumping water from the river up to the village tank on the hillside. There was a scuffling in the ceiling. That lizard really was getting too big.

A rooster crowed. Others answered, from every backyard. A donkey hee-hawed. A love song burst out of the radio—LOUDLY. Lights went on next door, and a different song blared from the neighbors' radio. The bus to Mazatlán started up and sat rumbling, waiting for the earliest passengers.

Lupe smelled the cooking tortillas and the coffee. She lifted the covers to get up, just as Angelica turned to her and said, "I bet you'd never climb that fig tree, Lupe. You're too scared of the ghost!"

Lupe didn't miss a beat. "Mmm," she yawned. "Just terrified. I guess I'll climb it after breakfast."

Luís heard the conversation, and he was terrified. "Lupe, don't!" he said.

"It's just superstition," she replied. "I like that old tree. You can climb it, too, Angelica. Then you can tell your friends you climbed a scary tree where a ghost lived by a cute, quaint, dirty, poor, boring village."

Angelica looked at her cousin. Maybe she had mentioned something about the village being quaint and cute a couple of times, but what was wrong with that? It *was*.

And it *was* mostly poor and dirty. And boring compared to the city. But Lupe sounded like she'd taken it all as a personal insult. How good it would be to be home again, where people understood her!

Angelica sighed and looked back up at the ceiling. There was enough light to see how pink the room was now—dark rosy pink. Above Tía Estela and Tío Ernesto's bed hung the painted crucifix and their wedding photograph in its silver frame.

"Sure, I'll climb it," she said, "after you."

So right after breakfast, Lupe, Luís, and Angelica followed the path to the river once again.

As Lupe walked along, she observed every house, every dog and bush and goat, every mud brick in every wall, and drank them into herself. She knew this village would never be boring or poor or dirty or anything but home to her. It was the only place she ever wanted to live.

As they got closer to the river, they could hear it gurgling quietly below the chirps of birds and the soft padding of their feet. The river was always there, underneath everything. How impossible it was for Angelica to understand, to know its different moods—its lazy trickle at the end of winter or its fury in spring. In springtime the rains poured on the Sierra Madres, sweeping tons of dirt from high in the mountains so that the streams churned thicker and thicker with mud, all surging into the wide, shallow river until it became a raging, deafening brown torrent that rolled great boulders down like marbles.

Last year, Lupe had found a tree half sunk in the flood and had climbed out onto its broad trunk. She was holding on to a branch that stuck up in the air and was bouncing along with the waves, when a neighbor had seen her and run to her father. Her father had raced down, helped her off, and marched her home, holding her wrist like a vise. It had turned black and blue the next morning, and Lupe rubbed it the whole time her father walked her back to the river where she stood next to him, staring, holding her swollen wrist. The tree was gone. Nothing was left but a gaping hole in the riverbank and the water that thundered in Lupe's ears.

Lupe smiled to herself as she remembered. That was the only other time her father had grounded her.

Angelica thought she'd be afraid to climb the tree of Señora Perez? She didn't know Lupe. She didn't know Lupe at all.

The three children reached the fig tree. Luís and Angelica sat on a rock in the sunlight.

"Watch out for rattlesnakes under there," Lupe said, and laughed as their legs shot into the air. She turned and walked into the shadow of the tree.

It was cool and quiet under the leaves. She looked up. The tree didn't feel scary at all—more like a woman with strong arms embracing the sky. Were they like the arms of Señora Perez? She couldn't remember. One branch curved out, thick and low to the ground. Lupe passed her hand over the smooth bark and pulled herself up.

This was an easy tree to climb. She climbed as high as she could, until the branches got too thin to go farther. She pulled the trunk so that it swayed back and forth with her weight.

"Nothing to it!" she called down. "Your turn next, Angelica!"

But she made no move to go down. She looked out over the dry land. From here she could see the hills rising away from the river. They were covered with the pale dry stalks of corn plants, the corn mostly harvested and stored for the winter. Her father was working in the fields somewhere, gathering the last of their crop. El Diablo would be tied nearby.

To a farmer, donkeys and mules are much more valuable than a horse. They are more surefooted, can carry much heavier loads, and are far less liable to get sick or hurt. But her father had wanted this horse, this stallion. He had never regretted buying him. And El Diablo was a prize.

Ever since the day three years ago when her father had brought him home, Lupe had helped to care for him and oil his saddle and bridle. He was named El Diablo, "the Devil," because he had been badly treated as a yearling and hated most adults. With her father and with children, especially with Lupe, he was gentle.

In the early months of the rainy season, when the ground was soft and the new green shoots were tender, Lupe would ride El Diablo to the hills where they could be alone. She would take off his saddle and bridle, and the two of them would pretend he was a wild stallion. He would race around, tossing his head and snorting, sometimes galloping close to Lupe, yet too far away for her to touch. Lupe would stand still as an owl, moving only her eyes, and wait.

At some point El Diablo would stop. He would amble over to nuzzle her, as though testing whether she was still alive. Lupe would spring onto his back and grip his mane.

Pretending to be frightened, the horse would race across the open space, stop, turn around and around, then rear up on his hind legs and paw the air until Lupe fell off.

Even when she hurt herself, Lupe hardly noticed. As El Diablo's hooves thundered away in triumph, she would lie on the wet ground, feeling the sound with her whole body, until the horse trotted back to her and blew his froth on her face. Lupe would laugh and throw her arms around his neck.

Once, her father had come upon them playing their game in the hills. He had only laughed, shaking his head as he brushed the dirt off her clothes. That was when he'd started calling her *Tigrilla Loca*—Crazy Little Tiger.

Lupe stood high in the tree and smiled, remembering.

It was time to go, time for Angelica's turn. Lupe began climbing down. The branches got thicker. Lupe went faster, dancing her way down.

See, Mama! I'm using my gift of a healthy body. I am dancing, dancing down!

Her foot slipped out from under her. She grabbed a branch, but her hand slid off.

Wait!

Hold on!

Branch!

But there was nothing to hold except air.

She reached and saw the leaves and branches moving by her, saw how the leaves were outlined in light against the morning sky, how on the larger branches, round scar spirals had formed over broken-off buds, saw how the branches seemed to move in waves as she went by them, and Lupe preserved every perfect detail in her memory.

She found herself on the ground at the bottom of the tree.

For a few moments she just lay there and breathed. Nothing hurt much. She pushed herself up to stand.

Pain burst from her back into her head, throwing her down against the dirt. She waited, took a breath, and tried to roll onto her back, but again the pain was crushing, like a giant force that pinned her down.

Toad. Poor old toad.

She lay still, gasping.

Why can't I move? Luís and Angelica are running toward me.

Luís and Angelica stopped next to Lupe, looking down at her legs, which lay in front of her, one crossed over the other, bent in strange positions. Lupe couldn't move them. She couldn't feel them. She looked up at Luís and Angelica. No one knew what to say.

CHAPTER FOUR

Lupe lay across the backseat of the bus, her head in her mother's lap. She watched the back of her father's head, in its white straw sombrero, and the top of Angelica's head, full of colored barrettes, jiggle above the seat back in front of her. She watched Luís sitting across the aisle from her, staring ahead. Lupe heard Flor begin to cry, felt her mother shift him so he could nurse, felt every bump as the bus drove over the rutted dirt road. No one looked at her or spoke.

The bus slowed to a stop, turned, and drove on, but smoothly now. They were on the highway to the city of Mazatlán, where a doctor would operate on Lupe's back and Angelica would return home. The wheels droned on the black tar. Lupe slept.

She woke as the bus was pulling into the station. Angelica jumped up and pushed her way out first. Lupe heard her calling, "Mommy! Daddy!" and thought she heard sobbing.

All she does is sob!

At least now she'll be gone.

Gone to her blue fountain.

Lupe's family stayed in their seats while the bus gradually emptied. Through the window, Lupe watched the driver hand down packages from the top of the bus: cloth bundles tied with rope, cardboard boxes, a basket full of chickens staring in different directions, a red chest with silver at the corners and a big gold lock in front. A bag of corn ripped as the driver passed it down, and the dark yellow ears began to fall out.

After the other passengers had left, Lupe's father picked up the two poles lying next to him on the floor. Her mother had sewn a cloth around the poles to make a stretcher. As gently as they could, they moved Lupe from the seat onto the stretcher. She bit into her stuffed bear to keep herself from screaming. Tears poured from her eyes before she could wipe them away.

They set her down on the cement platform while the two families hugged each other. Then Tía Gloria knelt down on the pavement in her white dress and gold necklaces and smoothed Lupe's hair and kissed her face, tears streaking her black eye makeup.

"I'm sorry, Lupita," she whispered. "I'm so very, very sorry." Her perfume mixed with the diesel fumes puffing from the buses all around them.

Angelica's dad hailed a taxi and helped lift Lupe into the backseat. He pulled a wad of money from his pocket and paid the driver, then hustled his wife and daughter

into a black Mercedes and drove off. Lupe's family piled themselves, and the food, water, and extra clothes they had brought, into the taxi and rode to the hospital.

Lupe was operated on almost immediately. After about an hour, her bed was rolled out of the operating room by three women in blue cotton coats. Lupe lay on top, pale and still. Her family had started to get up and follow her when the doctor walked out.

The doctor pulled his white coat together over his plump belly and paused, looking down his stubby nose at Lupe's father. Then the doctor jerked his chin up, just the tiniest bit, as a sign to her father that he should come with him. Ernesto stood up and followed the doctor through the halls.

They stopped at the entrance to the hospital, where an armed guard and a secretary sat behind an old wooden desk. The desktop was adorned with scratches, a telephone, and nothing else. The doctor stopped and turned to her father.

"Your daughter broke her back and is paralyzed from the waist down," he said bluntly. "There is nothing more to be done. She should stay here to recuperate for at least two weeks. You'll need to pay the full amount here at the

desk. The child will not be permitted to leave until the bill is paid."

The doctor knew he would not be seeing Lupe again and that she would almost certainly die of pressure sores within a few months. As a young man, he had worked day and night to save every patient who had fallen, crashed, been burned, shot, beaten, or infected with disease. But the public hospitals had too little money, and too many people came too late. Too often he had seen families ruined as they paid for a patient who died as soon as they went home. He was tired, tired of caring so much and being so discouraged. Now he only did his job, got his paycheck, and kept his feelings out of it. By the time he turned the corner, he was thinking about lunch.

Lupe's father watched the doctor's white coat grow smaller and smaller in the empty hall. He was thinking of the things his family owned. The operation had cost thousands of pesos. Angelica's father, his own rich brother, had offered no help. They would have to sell everything. The sound of his footsteps bounced back at him from the walls as he walked, searching for Lupe's room. He came in only to say good-bye to his wife and son and kiss Lupe on her forehead, then left at once for the village. Lupe was fast asleep and could not see the desolation in his eyes.

CHAPTER FIVE

The days passed and Lupe's father did not return. It would take him some time to get all the money for the operation.

Lupe was weak and tired but otherwise seemed fine. She talked and played quietly with Luís and Flor. She ate almost normally at first, then less and less. Her mother crocheted, and changed the towels under her when they got wet.

One day Tía Gloria walked in. Angelica followed behind her like a shrunken shadow, looking at the floor. Tía Gloria handed a big bouquet of flowers and two books to Lupe, comics and soccer magazines to Luís, and a bag of beautiful new yarn to Estela. She sat on the bed and held Lupe's hand. She talked about the family, about food and TV programs and politics and whatever else came into her head.

Angelica stood pressing herself against the wall and didn't say a word. She had changed completely. She wore no makeup and no earrings or other jewelry. Her hair was pulled back with a rubber band, and her plain dark blue dress came down below her knees. If she hadn't been with her mother, Lupe would never have recognized her. She almost looked like a nun. Angelica bit her lips, twisted her fingers together, and stared at Lupe with eyes full of fear.

As Lupe listened to her aunt and occasionally glanced over at her cousin, she felt her mind drift. She didn't notice anything unusual until all of a sudden she seemed to have floated up to the ceiling. Lupe found herself looking down on all of them. Her own body, lying down there in the bed, looked very tired. Her mind felt very clear, and into her head came the words *Nobody is to blame.*

Just as suddenly as she had floated up, Lupe was back inside her body again.

When Tía Gloria paused to take a breath, Lupe turned to her cousin.

"Forget it, Angelica," she said. "It wasn't your fault. It wasn't a ghost. I just came down too fast."

For a flicker of time, Angelica looked straight into Lupe's eyes. Then she looked back at the floor. Lupe let her eyelids close.

"Lupe is right, Angelica," Estela said. "She's a daredevil, a *Tigrilla Loca.* That's her nature. She just came down too fast."

Lupe felt her aunt squeeze her hand, and very soon she felt her stand up. Lupe opened her eyes in time to see the back of Angelica's dress vanish out the door. She saw Tía

Gloria kiss Luís, then take an envelope from her handbag and slip it into her mother's hand. After one quick hug, Tía Gloria followed her daughter out.

Estela opened the envelope, looked inside, counted, and burst into tears. "Thank God!" she whispered. "We might not lose the house!" She ran to call Señora Montez, whose grocery store had the only phone in the village.

Several days later Estela was changing the towels under Lupe when she noticed how big her daughter's belly had grown. The child looked like she was pregnant! At once she realized that Lupe had not gotten rid of any solid waste since the accident—almost two weeks earlier!

How could her daughter have a bowel movement when she couldn't feel anything and had no control over any muscles below her waist? Estela asked a nurse what to do.

"Oh," the nurse replied. "Everybody who's paralyzed has the same problem. We don't deal with that here. I can give you the name and address of a private nurse who specializes in elimination. She lives on the other side of town."

The following day Lupe's mother walked off through the unfamiliar city streets. Late in the afternoon she returned with the nurse. The woman put on plastic gloves, greased her finger, and went to work. Thirteen days after the accident, Lupe's waste was pulled out onto sheets of newspaper that had been spread on the bed.

The nurse taught Lupe how to do this and how to let her urine out into a plastic bag. Lupe learned how to clean the plastic gloves and tubes so she could take care of everything by herself every day. She did it all well. She also wanted to disappear into the blue hospital walls.

The day after the nurse's visit, her father returned with the rest of the money they needed. He paid, and they were free to go.

Few people noticed the family as they walked back through the city to the bus station—Lupe's father holding the stretcher in front, her mother and Luís behind. Everything was piled on top around their daughter, who lay taking in the delights of Mazatlán. Cars and trucks rumbled by and honked. The sidewalks were uneven and crowded with people, so Lupe was jostled and jerked as she lay powerless, looking up. The buildings were tall and dirty and full of windows reflecting the glare of the sun. The sun beat down from a gray-white sky that smelled of food and diesel fumes and was crisscrossed everywhere by black electric wires.

How can Angelica describe this place as clean and beautiful? Is her part of the city so different?

When they finally got to the station, Lupe's family laid her on the ground and sat, exhausted and sweating. Estela unwrapped a stack of tortillas. They ate without speaking and waited to go home.

The bus drove back over the smooth asphalt and bumpy dirt, past the same villages, up into the familiar hills. Lupe noticed the other passengers staring at her with pity, or sneaking embarrassed glances when they thought she wasn't looking. She felt like some strange animal, and she snuggled close to her father, hoping he would joke and laugh and cheer her up. Her father kept

his eyes on the moving world outside the window and said nothing.

When the sky was that pure, clear, purplish blue it gets just before nightfall, and the village streets echoed with quiet sounds, Lupe's family got off the bus. They passed windows and open doors that glowed yellow and blue-white from lightbulbs and televisions. The neighbors were inside getting supper ready and didn't see them carry Lupe by on their way home.

Estela turned on the lights as they carried her through the front room to the veranda surrounding the central garden. Their cat, Micho, jumped onto the stretcher. Lupe held him and blinked in the glare. Something was very wrong.

The rooms were almost empty. The television was gone. The great old table and chairs her father's grand-father had carved, the envy of the village—gone. Her mother's high carved bureau and the cupboard—gone. Their clothes and plates were stacked on the floor next to the year's supply of corn.

Lupe looked in the corner for El Diablo's gear. A little spider scuttled delicately across the empty floor.

CHAPTER SIX

For the first couple of weeks after they came back, the house was constantly full of friends and neighbors stopping by to visit and bring food. They would all sit around the bed out on the veranda and talk with Estela about the accident, the hospital—and how much it had all cost. When Estela tried to change the conversation, the visitors would invariably turn to Lupe, smiling brightly and patting her hand with great sympathy, and ask her how she felt.

Lupe didn't really feel any different. She just couldn't walk. But when she tried to tell people this, they would shake their heads and sigh, and offer a helpful comment like: "We all have our cross to bear" or "Everything happens for a reason" or "Poor child. At least you can use your hands. Maybe it's time to take up knitting."

At the beginning, Lupe talked with everybody, as she always had. But as day after day filled with looks of pity, kisses of pity, and voices sugary with pity, Lupe withdrew. After a couple of weeks Lupe merely nodded her head when someone spoke to her, and she lay alone hour after hour in the empty rooms. Hour by hour she came to understand what her one misstep had taken away.

She continued to take care of herself, but she was getting very tired and weak. She ate less and less. Finally she stopped talking to anyone, even her family.

• • •

Lupe lay in bed and smelled the tortillas and beans cooking. She heard her brother teasing Flor. The noise got on her nerves, but she was too tired to do anything about it. She felt so hot—tired and hot. She lay looking at the garden her mother tended so carefully. Estela loved to spend time watering the plants or picking off dead leaves or sweeping the winding brick walkway. Each bush or fern overflowed the sides of its own pot or was surrounded by a circle of painted white stones. Estela's favorite Rose of Many Surprises climbed up onto the roof, each rose a different hue.

As Lupe stared out, she began to hate every plant in the garden. They didn't do anything but sit and look stupid, stuck tight in the dirt. Stuck, stuck, stuck. She looked at the poinsettia tree. Skinny and scraggly, its red flowers seemed to glow hot and reach out for her, moving ever closer until they felt like burning tongues inside her head.

Estela came to the bed and felt Lupe's forehead. Her head, her whole body, was burning with fever. She had felt a little hot soon after she had come back from the hospital, then she had grown feverish in the afternoons. Last

35

night she had woken up in a sweat, throwing off the blanket and drinking the whole bottle of water beside her bed. Estela had given her cold drinks and put cold cloths on her forehead and neck, hoping the fever would go away, but today Lupe was burning. And still silent.

Estela called Señora Alvarez, the healer. When people were most worried and had no idea what to do, they always called Señora Alvarez. The old woman examined Lupe and asked her a few questions. She and Estela turned her onto her stomach so that the healer could give Lupe a shot. It was then she noticed the swollen dark patch of skin at the base of her spine. Señora Alvarez put the syringe back into her bag, unused.

"Estela," she said, "your daughter is very sick. I have seen this twice before. Both times the person died. Your daughter's skin is rotting inside, because she cannot move and because the bed is pressing against her here. That is what has given her the fever. I cannot help her, but I know of a place that can. Estela, you must take her to the center for disabled people. It is in a village like ours, in these mountains. You must take her there or she will die very soon."

After Señora Alvarez left, Lupe's mother stood by the bed and looked down at her sleeping daughter. How the family had changed in these few weeks since the accident! Lupe's father spent little time at home now, stopping at the bar every night for two or three hours. Instead of playing outside with his friends, Luís sat on the floor and played marbles alone. Flor seemed to cry and whine all the time. And this little girl, this wonderful crazy little tiger who had been so lively, always laughing and talking and moving like a restless wind, now only lay and stared at the garden. When her friend Ana had come to play with her, Lupe closed her eyes and turned away. Ana no longer stopped by.

As Estela stood over her, Lupe opened her eyes, looked up at her mother, and spoke. Her voice was clear and calm. "Mama," she said. "I've decided I want to die. You've had to sell everything because of me, even El Diablo. I'm a cripple forever. When I'm dead, you can have another baby who's whole."

Estela felt the pit of her stomach go cold.

Carefully, she lowered herself onto the edge of the bed. She took Lupe's hand—so hot, soft, and little—in both of hers, and looked into her daughter's eyes.

"Lupe, treasure," she said, "you are the daughter we want. We still have our house, and one field. We still have one another. We loved you the way you were before. We love you just as much the way you are now. But we need you to work on getting better."

Lupe kept her eyes on her mother's face the whole time she spoke. She seemed to be looking for a sign she couldn't find, listening for words that didn't come. As soon as her mother stopped speaking, Lupe closed her eyes and said nothing more.

Estela was so very tired. Everything had turned out so badly! Even as she spoke to Lupe, her own words felt hollow to her, inadequate. If only Lupe could get well!

Instead, she was growing weaker. She ate almost nothing. She hated the world. The only time she showed any life was when Micho jumped onto the bed and purred into her neck. Then Lupe would hug the cat and cry with no sound, her whole body trembling.

Estela wondered how this center for the disabled could help. The surgery had done nothing, and the expense had ruined them.

She bowed her head and prayed.

The next day she saw that the dark patch just above Lupe's bottom had broken open. The flesh inside looked gray and dead. As Estela washed the area, a mass of black goo pulled away, leaving a wide hole. Lupe said nothing as her mother cleaned the sore. It didn't hurt at all; she only felt her mother doing something to her back. But a rotten and disgusting smell filled the room. Lupe knew it came from something inside of her. She was sure it had taken over her whole body.

* * *

She was hardly aware when her father lifted her onto the bus, changed to another bus and yet another, and carried her through the streets of a strange village. She heard a metal gate squeak as it opened, heard her father talking and her name mentioned several times. The sounds were all dulled, as though they were taking place in another world. She felt herself being lowered into a chair, but she kept her eyes closed to shut out the light, the world.

"*Hola,* Lupe."

The woman's low voice was so close, Lupe felt breath on her face.

Mint toothpaste and coffee.

Perfume?

Lupe opened her eyes. Two green, almond-shaped eyes

looked back at her, two green eyes in a pale brown face surrounded by exploding brown clouds of hair. Below the eyes, the mouth was smiling.

Lupe thought the woman must be an angel. *I must have died,* she told herself, *and now I am in heaven.*

CHAPTER SEVEN

Lupe stared at the beautiful woman sitting in front of her. Then she saw her father standing beside the woman.

He's wearing normal clothes. I thought everybody in heaven wore white robes.

A crow cawed. Closer by, a pig squealed.

They wouldn't have crows and pigs in heaven, would they?

Am I still alive?

But if I'm still alive, where am I?

Lupe observed the woman more carefully.

Something was very peculiar. Lupe had some trouble figuring out what it was, but once she did, she realized it was quite simple. The woman didn't pity her. Her friends and family treated her with pity, and she expected the rest of the world to do the same. After all, she was crippled, and probably dying.

But this woman was smiling at her with pleasure, as though this was a normal meeting, as though Lupe was a normal, healthy girl. The woman just seemed glad to meet her.

"Lupe, my name is María," the woman said. "You're in a new place now. Everybody who lives here got hurt in some way, just like you did. Our bodies don't work like everybody else's. Here we learn to take care of ourselves—and to take care of one another."

Lupe said nothing.

María looked up at a big man with a round gentle face who stood on the other side of her, leaning on metal crutches. "This is Adrián, Lupe. The two of us will take care of you today, and we'll all take turns until you're well again."

Energy seemed to burst from Lupe's chest and flow out to the tips of her fingers. She could even feel it leaking down to her toes. *Well again?*

Lupe's head popped off the back of the chair, and she sat bolt upright.

For the second time in two days, she spoke.

"Well again? I'll be able to walk?"

María smiled—and shook her head.

"No, Lupe. You won't be able to walk, but you'll go wherever you want in a wheelchair, like I do. Look!"

María glided away, whirled around, and glided back, all in a few seconds.

Lupe stared. As suddenly as it had appeared, the energy drained from her body.

Hopeless after all.

This woman with the smiley face is in a wheelchair. A cripple. Not normal at all.

How dare she act normal, then? How dare she smile?

She's crippled, crippled!

Lupe squeezed the arms of the chair as hard as she could. She felt her hands shaking. She looked down at them, hoping she was squashing the chair into pulp—and noticed something worse.

Lupe herself was in a wheelchair.

Terrified, she looked around. In the large courtyard beyond her father, people were walking about on crutches and riding in wheelchairs. One man zipped along in a bizarre tricycle wagon. A little boy with golden curls—who actually did look like an angel, except he was wearing a turquoise T-shirt and red shorts that were quite dirty—was moving toward her, pushing a little wooden stand with wooden wheels. It squeaked. Lupe thought it sounded like a dying baby bird. How could anybody pretend this was normal!

Sure isn't heaven!

Nightmare!

SQUEAK, SQUEAK, SQUEAK! The boy roll-walked over to them and stopped next to Lupe's father. He didn't even come up to her father's belt. The boy stared at her, friendly and curious. Lupe glared back. One more happy cripple! She'd be better off dead.

She shut her eyes and lay back. She saw herself wrapped in a white sheet covered with flowers, riding El Diablo into the sky. Angels in long white robes sat on clouds, playing harps and holding their arms out to her. As

soon as El Diablo touched a cloud, Lupe leaped off and started dancing, throwing flowers that floated over all the other angels and horses dancing with her.

Nothing happened. Nobody said anything or went anywhere. Lupe opened her eyes again. Now she noticed that María was wearing pale green eye shadow. Eye shadow? On a cripple? Lupe was furious. She wanted to get OUT of here.

She grabbed the arms of the chair and suddenly pushed herself up, lunging forward out of the seat. María and Adrián caught her, and Adrián and her father settled her back into the wheelchair.

Her father held her arms.

"LUPE!"

María burst out laughing. "Well, that was a healthy jump there, Tiger!" she said, rubbing her arm. "Here we thought you were almost dead, and you're trying to fly! I think it's time we take you to the clinic and look at your pressure sore now. We have to clean it up and treat it so you can start to heal. But take this pill first. It's an antibiotic to fight all those bacteria trying to take over your body."

Lupe gave up. She swallowed the pill, closed her eyes, and let her arms and head flop down. People could do what they wanted with her. She felt herself being wheeled through the courtyard, felt the hot sun change to shade, and heard the rumbling of the wheels become a quiet hiss as they rolled onto a concrete floor. She felt herself lifted out of the chair and laid flat on her stomach on something soft.

The squeak of little wooden wheels followed her all the way.

CHAPTER EIGHT

The pressure sore on Lupe's back wasn't pretty. It was full of pus and blood, and it was oozing around the edges. María took a pair of plastic gloves out of their wrapping of brown paper towels and began to clean the sore with little squares of gauze.

Maybe it was the strange new surroundings, or maybe she had slept so long on the bus she had gotten some energy back, but whatever the reason, Lupe was a bit more awake now. The situation presented a great quandary for her, though. She was actually very, very curious about what was going on, but she didn't want anybody to know, so she kept her eyes closed and squinted through her eyelashes. This alone kept her from seeing much. In addition, her vision was blocked by Adrián's generous belly, which she could see, encased in its red plaid shirt, moving back and forth under her arm. And she couldn't feel anything, except that her body started jiggling more and more against the bed.

Are they jumping up and down on me?

Are they pounding things into me?

Adrián moved a little to the side, and Lupe saw a couple of used pads drop onto the floor. They were soaking wet and stained a mix of red and grayish yellow. María's hand held out a clean pad to Adrián. He poured brown liquid onto it, and María went back to making Lupe's body jiggle. As María glanced down at Lupe's face, she noticed the little quiver of her eyelashes, so she politely ignored Lupe's pretense of sleep and started talking. "This brown liquid Adrián just poured on the pad is soap, Lupe. I'm washing the inside of your pressure sore. I've been scrubbing all around the bone and down under the edges of the skin—sort of like scrubbing dirty dishes. Now it's all clean, and I'm rinsing away the soap with boiled water."

Lupe was quite happy to get this explanation, but there was no way she was going to let anybody know this, so she kept pretending to be asleep—wondering at the same time why María acted as though she was awake.

Adrián walked away on his crutches and picked up a big plastic jar. When he moved off, Lupe saw her father sitting on a chair behind him, fast asleep. Her father really was asleep. His mouth was open, and he was snoring lightly. His chest rose and fell as he breathed. Lupe looked at the wide brown hands that held his hat on his knees. The edges of his sleeves were frayed. She looked at the rim around his head where the hat had flattened his hair.

When had he gotten all those gray hairs? When had the lines in his face sunk in so deep?

Adrián came back with the jar and spooned out gobs of gold-colored guck onto the white squares that María held out.

Lupe kept her eyes almost closed. María kept on talking. "This is a mixture of honey and sugar, Lupe. We're packing the sore with it. You know how mold never grows on honey? Well, sugar-honey stops bacteria from growing on your sore, too, and it stops the cells from swelling up. Now your sick cells can recover and the healthy cells around the sore can stay strong. We'll do this twice a day until you're well."

Lupe no longer felt any jiggling, but only some pushing, as María stuffed the sugar-honey–covered pads into the hole and Adrián taped a gauze patch onto it. Then she felt the sheet being pulled up over her back. María and Adrián closed the bottles and put everything away. As they were sweeping up the floor underneath her, Lupe drifted off to sleep.

She woke as Adrián and her father were lifting her onto a foam mattress made of lots of soft little peaks like the insides of egg cartons.

"You'll have to stay on your stomach for a while so your back can heal without that pressure on it," Adrián said. "This new bed of yours is a gurney—a bed on wheels. It's your own private car that you can drive wherever you want. Try it. Push these front wheels with your hands."

Lupe pushed. The whole bed rolled forward.

"Watch out, Lupe," Adrián said. "If you're not careful,

that smile's going to crawl out over your whole face and take over."

He was right. It was one weak smile, but it was there. Lupe immediately frowned, stared straight ahead, and rolled out to the courtyard. Her father and Adrián walked beside her, into the sunlight.

She rolled smoothly along next to the playground built in the middle of the courtyard. Like a blue lake in the middle of a desert, the playground was impossible to miss. Swings and parallel bars and seesaws and a jungle gym, all painted in wild colors, stood empty and waiting. Lupe barely gave them a glance. She couldn't use any of those things anymore, and besides, she was too old for that childish stuff.

Then she saw the two giant rocking horses, and her hands grabbed the wheels so hard her body pitched forward, then fell back on the bed, while she stared.

The rocking-horse bodies were old tires tied up on wooden posts. Their heads were flat boards nailed to sticks that poked up through the tires. One horse was actually a cow, with horns. Each head was painted with round white eyes and big teeth. They were the ugliest, stupidest-looking, most wonderful rocking horses she'd ever seen.

They also reminded her of El Diablo, and everything she had lost. She pushed the wheels forward, scowling.

"Where will I stay?"

Adrián raised his eyebrows but made no comment, and led her to a bright green room crowded with beds, clothes, radios, posters, stuffed animals, and makeup.

"You'll be sharing this with three roommates," he said. "They're out working now, but they'll be back in a while. Make yourself comfortable. I'll see you soon."

Lupe's dad put her bag of clothes down in the one empty spot on the floor. He looked around, then took out her clothes and hairbrush, toothbrush and toothpaste, her stuffed brown musical bear and white cat, her box with the three horses, and arranged them all on a shelf. Lupe thought he seemed uncomfortable, even though he was being quite efficient with all this arranging business. Maybe it was because this was her mom's job, and he didn't know how to do it very well?

"That's exactly how I like it, Papa," she reassured him. "They look good there."

Her father put the empty bag next to the wall, then turned toward Lupe, looking at her with a strange sort of embarrassed expression. He rubbed his hands against his legs a couple of times, and cleared his throat.

Suddenly, Lupe understood what was going on. He was going to leave her here—alone. That's what she got for talking.

She stared back at him, shaking her head. *No. No.*

He walked toward her, but she backed the gurney away until it hit the wall. He stopped and stood in the middle of the jumbled room.

"I have to leave now, *mi Tigrilla*," he said. "The people here will take good care of you."

He came to her, leaned over and smoothed her hair back, pushed a loose strand behind her ear.

"We will come a week from Sunday, in twelve days. Be

51

wise." He took her face in both his big dry hands, kissed her forehead, her cheeks, her mouth—then left.

Lupe watched him walk away in his black pants, gray jacket, white hat. She felt her chest rise and fall against the puffy bed and remembered his chest rising and falling as he sat on the chair, asleep. Her throat hurt. She rolled to the doorway and peeked out in time to see him close the gate, turn, wave, and disappear.

Lupe felt nothing. Nothing at all. Everything was blank. In spite of what he had said, in spite of everything she knew, she was sure her father was never coming back. She was trapped here at this Home for Happy Cripples.

She let her head fall on the pillow and watched nothing happen to the painted green wall, until at last her eyes closed, and she truly slept.

CHAPTER NINE

Lupe didn't notice her three roommates come in, quietly play the radio and talk, change into nightclothes, and finally turn off the light and get into bed. She hardly noticed the two times someone came in during the night to give her a pill. She slept for hours, a black, dreamless, healing sleep.

She woke to see a small skinny woman doing something with her hands as she lay in a bed across the room. The woman was holding a mirror close to her face. It didn't take Lupe long to see that she was pulling hairs out of her eyebrows. She kept plucking until they were perfect arches, like black rainbows. The woman's long fingers were twisted together into bony white paws. She put the mirror down and pulled off the covers. Every movement she made was jerky. When she had finally twisted herself out of bed, Lupe saw that she was still bent way over.

The woman saw Lupe watching her.

"*Hola,* Lupe," she said. "I'm Rosario. Arthritis—if I don't exercise, I get stiff as a board. Wait till I dress. We'll have breakfast."

Breakfast. It was light outside. At home, breakfast would be over by now. Lupe imagined her dad leaving for the cornfields. With El Diablo gone, he'd have to walk out there now, his machete over his shoulder. Rosario picked up a pink T-shirt. On the front was a picture of a blue ocean full of fish outlined in silver glitter, with *Cape Cod* written across it in fluorescent green letters. She pulled it over her head, slowly, jerkily, pulled on a pair of pink pants over her bony white legs. Luís would be in school now, drawing pictures of cars in his geography notebook. Rosario combed her black hair and put on sparkling earrings and red lipstick. Mama would be nursing Flor or maybe sweeping the walkway in the garden.

Do they ever think of me?

The two other women were just getting up as Rosario walked out. The familiar smells of tortillas, beans, and coffee floated across the sunny courtyard. Rosario swayed from side to side as she walked. Lupe rolled smoothly behind her, noticing.

The first thing she noticed in the cafeteria was not the woman frying frijoles at the stove, or the long tables where people were eating as they sat in their wheelchairs or on the benches with their crutches beside them. Her eyes swept by them all, but she didn't really see them. What Lupe noticed was a man in the corner where there wasn't much light, lying on a gurney, like she was. Two pretty women were feeding him.

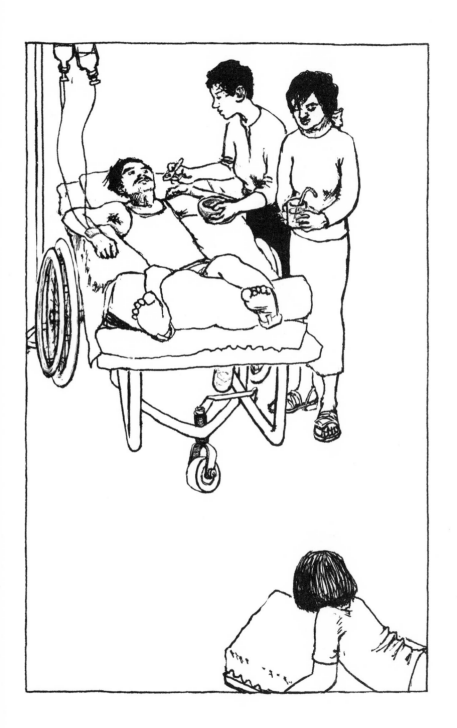

Rosario saw Lupe staring. "That's Martín. He was at a soccer game and fell off the bleachers from high up. Broke his neck. Quadriplegic—can't move anything but his head. Those are his sisters, here about a week. Think your pressure sore was bad, Lupe? Martín had two giant ones, real deep. Almost killed him all over again. Lucky he's got sisters to take care of him."

Lupe was wondering how Rosario knew about her pressure sore, when Martín turned his head and looked at her. His face was as handsome as a movie star's, with a thick black mustache and dark, kind eyes. Lupe felt her stomach melt. She and Martín stared at each other for several seconds. Lupe lowered her head and pushed the gurney to the breakfast table. She felt her hands on the wheels, felt her back as it arched up, felt her chest against the mattress. For the first time since the accident, Lupe felt lucky.

After breakfast she followed Rosario to the porch, where the boy with the curls sat at the foot of a bed, playing with two ropes that hung from the ceiling.

"*Hola,* José!" Rosario called out. "Time to help me before school?"

He nodded. Rosario wriggled onto the bed and picked up the other ends of the ropes. Lupe looked up and saw that the ropes went through some pulleys in the ceiling. She saw them straighten as José pulled, and Rosario's head and chest lifted up. José raised his arms. Rosario fell back again. Up, down, up, down, over and over and over.

Lupe watched, confused.

All that work she does, just to keep moving? Why doesn't she just give up?

José's so little, and she's big, and he's helping her!

56

He's just a little crippled child!

Rosario let go of the ropes. "Off to school now, José, or you'll be late. Go!"

School?

José slid down from the bed, grabbed his walker, and pushed off, squeak-squeak-squeaking across the courtyard and out the gate.

As Lupe watched his perky little body move off with its perky little drag-step-step-drag of a walk, she felt hatred well up in her stomach and fill her throat like a hot, solid mass. She almost choked with it. Lupe had never hated anybody this much in her life, not even Angelica.

As José pulled the gate closed behind him, the squeak seemed to pierce right into Lupe's bones.

Cripple! Cripple! Cripple! Cripples are outside of life, and sad, like I am.

José's always happy!

Cripples can't do anything. They need help. But José helps other people—even grown-ups.

I'm stuck inside this jail. José gets to leave whenever he wants.

He's free!

And his stupid wheels squeak! They drive me nuts!

That afternoon, after her dressing had been changed, Lupe lay on her gurney out on the porch. Under a tree in the middle of the courtyard, a woman sat in a wheelchair at a big outdoor sink, washing clothes. Suddenly Lupe saw herself and her mom washing clothes at the river. Lupe was flicking sprays of water at Flor to make him laugh. Her mom's arms were covered in soapsuds, and she was smiling, smiling, smiling.

Lupe shook her head and shut her eyes, but the memory wouldn't go away. She put her head on her arms. The tears poured out. They slid down her nose, her arms, and onto the sheet.

Something squeaked. Lupe looked up. José stood a few paces away, calmly watching her, his angelic little head cocked to one side.

"Go away!" she shrieked. "JUST GO AWAY!"

CHAPTER TEN

For the next few days, Lupe mostly slept. Her dressings and her clothes were changed, she was fed and given antibiotics. She refused to let anyone help with her elimination. But mostly Lupe wheeled herself slowly around the compound, and watched, and slept. And gradually she began to heal.

One afternoon, Lupe was dozing on the veranda. SKREEEEEK! The gates flew open. A flock of children raced inside—normal children who could run and jump and climb and do whatever they wanted.

What are they doing here?

Most of them ran straight for the playground. Two boys climbed onto the rocking horses and bounced back and forth, whooping and yelling.

Oh, the playground.

Lupe wanted nothing to do with that place. She turned the gurney away.

A few of the children walked past the playground and into a shed near the clotheslines. Once they were all inside, Lupe cautiously rolled after them. The door of the shed was open. All she could see were the silhouettes of children moving around. She smelled wood, freshly cut wood. She rolled a little way inside.

Kids, some machines, a man on a gurney.
I've seen him around, know his name: Jorge.
Cupboards full of wood, cans of paint . . .
What are those things stacked on benches?
They look like . . . wooden puzzles and toys.
This is a toy shop?
Here?

Trying to be invisible, Lupe wheeled herself closer. Two girls were sanding slices of wood. A boy was drawing on tracing paper. Jorge was watching a girl with dark curly hair as she guided a square of wood through a jigsaw. The saw blade was a thin vertical blur, and it whined as it sliced through the outline of a cat. The girl turned the wood to cut the final curve of the tail. Her whole body was fixed on that one point where the line met the saw blade. Carefully, intently, she guided the wood back through the slit out to the edge. Done!

She turned off the saw. The whine still buzzed in Lupe's ears. The girl held the cut puzzle out to Jorge. Jorge twisted a few thin hairs of his drooping mustache, nodded, then wheeled over to two boys who were painting wooden circles.

Lupe felt she had been doing a good job of being invisible, when the girl at the saw looked straight at her and smiled.

"Want to try?" she asked. Lupe was so surprised, she didn't know what to do. So she nodded. "Uh, sure. Yes, I do."

"You have to be really careful of the saw blade," the girl said. "It'll slice through your fingers easier than it does through the wood. Just keep them out of the way."

Sounded reasonable. Lupe nodded again.

"My name's Ivette. What's yours?"

"Uh, Guadalupe. Lupe."

Ivette found a large scrap of wood and drew a curvy line on it.

"Don't start it right at the saw blade, or it'll jump around," Ivette said. "Let the blade get up speed first. Just remember: Guide it more than push. And let it go slowly."

She turned on the machine. The blade whined and became a blur. Ivette moved the wood part of the way in, then pulled it out and let Lupe try. Jorge glanced over, then went back to helping the boys.

The wood was easy to cut. It almost melted away. But she had trouble staying on the line.

Guide more than push.

Easier said than done.

Ivette didn't say anything, just stood and watched. With one hand on either side of the singing blade, Lupe cut all the way through.

Ivette showed her where to turn off the saw. They looked at Lupe's cut. It was crooked and off the pencil line.

"Not bad," Ivette said. "Lots better than my first try."

Lupe and Ivette worked for a couple of hours, until Ivette had to go home.

"See you soon, Lupe." She ran off.

Lupe rolled outside and lay in the late afternoon sun. She was tired. She was also sort of . . . happy.

Ivette.

Everything was quiet except for a faint rippling noise—a noise so familiar to Lupe that she hadn't noticed it before. She rolled toward it.

At the far edge of the courtyard stood a hedge made up of tall prickly cactus trees. Lupe wheeled up to the spiky hedge and looked through. Just beyond, a steep cliff fell down to a river, just like the one that flowed by her own village. She could almost see the same dark red and blue and speckled rocks. They made the same hollow knocking sound as the water wore them smooth.

Across the river, three men and a donkey walked along a path. The donkey was loaded with sacks of corn. They waded into the water and crossed to Lupe's side, then disappeared below the cliff. Maybe one of the men was Ivette's father, going home.

Home. Lupe lay on the gurney and watched the sparkling water until the purple shadows of the mountains moved over the river and the fields of corn. Silently the shadows slid up the cliff and over the courtyard until they covered the center and the village around it.

CHAPTER ELEVEN

The next morning, Lupe lay on her gurney in the court-yard, thinking about Ivette. Ivette had treated her like a regular person, a normal, old . . . friend. Lupe sighed.

In front of her, Juan lumbered by. Juan was a great big sort of boy-man, always flopping around from room to room in hopes of some new task.

"Job?" he'd ask. "Job for Juan?"

He was so strong that he could easily lift people who couldn't move themselves. Whenever there was something heavy to carry, people would call, "Juan! Juan!" and he'd lunge forth to help.

Lupe heard a loud sort of moan from the patio across from her. That was Gustavo. "Unnnhhh!" he bellowed. His spidery, stiff limbs were shooting out in all directions like wild sticks, waving at Juan. Lupe watched Juan smile, turn, and barge across the courtyard to him.

"Walk?" he asked. "Want a walk?"

Gustavo waved his arms and legs around some more and moaned louder. Juan leaned Gustavo's wheelchair back a little and pushed him purposefully off across the courtyard and out the gate. Lupe watched them go.

Are they friends?

What else would you call it?

A couple of chickens fluttered down from the trees where they had spent the night and started pecking on the ground. They didn't seem to pay any attention to each other, but they didn't go very far away from each other, either. They reminded Lupe of the way Luís acted with some of his friends. They'd walk along the river for hours exploring, or they'd hang out at home, not saying a word. Lupe had always thought this was a very odd way for friends to act. Maybe it was just . . . different.

Two black pigs raced through the courtyard, squealing. They passed right in front of Lupe and disappeared into the bushes. Were animals friends with each other? Had she been friends with El Diablo? She knew she loved him, but were they friends?

A little beyond the chickens, María sat at the outdoor sink, scrubbing a sheet. It was a very unusual sink, made of concrete and set on a base of bricks that came up just high enough so that somebody could roll a wheelchair underneath and scrub clothes to his or her heart's content. Lupe wondered if "heart's content" was exactly the expression to use with "washing clothes," but María did seem to be quite . . . content.

Lupe rolled over next to her. María rinsed the soapsuds away with a hose, squeezed out the sheet, tossed it into a plastic bucket, and reached for the next one. María kept washing sheets. Lupe kept watching her. The sun filtered down through the leaves of the tree. Cicadas buzzed.

María picked up the bucket and rolled over to the clothesline. It was way too high for her to reach. Martín's sister Dolores was hanging up laundry. She smiled and took the bucket from María. María and Lupe sat watching her hang up the sheets one by one.

"When I first found out my legs didn't work," María said, "I turned right into a puddle. I stayed in a dark room and hated the world. I couldn't do anything. Two years like that. Then I came here. Now there's nothing I can't do." She laughed. "Well, almost nothing. I can't reach up high."

Dolores hung the last sheet, handed the bucket to María, and left.

"Maybe that's the lesson I've learned here," María said. "We can do everything, if each one of us does what we can. But we all need one another to stay alive. A few people want to 'help' us, which means they want to feed us and dress us and wipe us off, and be kind by doing everything for us, so we lose any way to be useful members of the human population. But most of society doesn't even want to help us; they just want us to disappear, like a big pimple on their nose. We remind people this could happen to them." She paused for a moment and looked at Lupe.

"So if we don't take care of one another and keep one another strong, watch out! This whole center will just be a bunch of dead or useless cripples!"

María laughed like she'd cracked the funniest joke in

the world. Lupe thought she was weird, and she felt extremely uncomfortable with all this graphic truth.

"Mama!" a high little voice yelled from the other side of the courtyard. "Mama! Mama!"

María turned.

"*Hola,* Lluvia, joy of my life!"

Adrián was walking toward them. Holding his hand and skipping along beside him was a little girl in a pink dress and white sandals with white lacy socks. Astounded, embarrassed, Lupe looked at María, who looked back at her and burst out laughing.

"I guess you didn't know, eh, Lupe? Adrián's my husband. This is our daughter, Lluvia. Disabled people really can do anything—even get married and have children!"

María lifted Lluvia onto the wheelchair and rolled off. Adrián walked beside them. He looked sort of like Lupe's father, walking away.

This was all a bit too much for Lupe to take. But she was *not* going to cry again, especially in front of people! She wheeled herself around behind the sheets, where nobody could see her.

Once she got there, she didn't feel like crying anymore. She rested her chin on her hands, listening to the river and gazing at the ground, the scattered leaves. Snuggled down in the brown roots of a tree sat a small brown toad.

Step on a toad and no rain for a year.
I'll squash it flat as a tortilla.
Angelica, face all wet with tears.
Stupid superstition!
Falling, falling, falling, falling, falling.
Poor old toad.

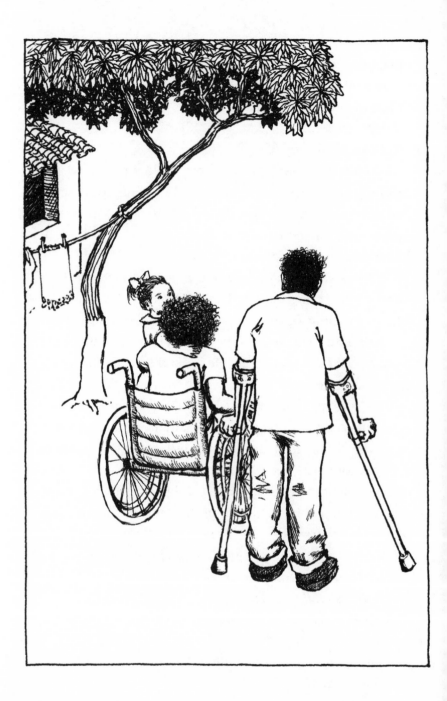

Lupe's dad had always told her that every creature played a special part in God's world, even if humans didn't understand how. She knew toads ate insects that ate people's vegetables. Maybe they did something else, too. Maybe they did keep the rain coming, just by being alive. Not by being perfect or whole—just alive.

Faintly, Lupe heard the squeak of wooden wheels. *Oh, no!* She closed her eyes and pretended to be asleep. The wheels came closer. She kept her eyes closed. The squeaking went by her and then away. She opened her eyes.

A puppy was waddling toward the cactus hedge. José was following it. The puppy walked through the hedge and stood at the edge of the cliff, sniffing and whimpering.

"Here, puppy," José called.

He let go of his walker and knelt down. He pushed himself through the spiky cactus on his knees. The spines caught his shirt. He pulled hard. The puppy moved sideways.

"Here, puppy."

He reached out—and fell over the cliff. He was gone.

"HELP!" Lupe yelled with all her might. "José fell over the cliff! Help! HEELLLP!"

CHAPTER TWELVE

Appearing and disappearing behind the sheets and clothes, María seemed to fly across the courtyard. Other people's shadows flickered fast over the ground and slipped up the sheets. The sheets parted, and people poured through: María and red-haired Consuela in their wheelchairs, Juan and Ramón and Martín's sisters running, Rosario hobbling, then others on crutches or on gurneys.

The puppy shot back through the hedge and raced into the courtyard, away from the crowd of frantic humans. José's walker lay on its side by the tall cactus hedge, looking small and alone. Then it was surrounded and hidden by legs and wheelchairs and bodies. Nobody could see through the hedge over the cliff. Nobody could tell what had happened to José.

Ramón tried to slide through a space between two cacti. They were too close. Martín's skinny sister, Dolores, bent down and wriggled through. People pulled the spines out of her clothes as she passed. She lay at the edge of the cliff and called down.

"Hey! José!"

Everybody listened.

"José! *Hola,* old man! You awake?"

A tiny voice floated up. "*Hola,* Dolores! You have a big scratch on your face!"

Everybody laughed, even Lupe.

José had fallen only partway down the cliff, onto a dirt ledge. Dolores climbed down, holding tight to a rope tied around a tree, and helped him climb back up. Everybody watched all evening and the next day to see if he might have a concussion, but he was fine.

People congratulated Lupe.

"Glad you never talked before, Lupe. We'd all be deaf."

"Gorgeous voice you've got there, Lupe! You'll be another Lola Beltrán!"

"Stick by me, Lupita! If I cut my finger, the whole village will come running!"

Lupe didn't say much, but she knew that under all the teasing people were actually praising her. If her legs didn't work, her voice sure did—when she wanted it to. And her hands, arms, eyes, and ears.

•   •   •

Lupe no longer slept most of the day. The medicine was killing the bacteria; her pressure sore was healing; and she was getting stronger. She decided to work on something at the toy workshop—a project of her own. Something for her father.

As soon as she thought of him, she knew exactly what she wanted to make. Maybe they would come on Sunday, like he'd said.

No. Get rid of that thought. They couldn't come even if they wanted to. There's no money left.

Just mail it to him.

Lupe wheeled herself to the workshop and told Jorge what she wanted to do. He handed her a small block of wood and a pencil. When she'd drawn the figure the way she wanted it, he helped her cut the basic shape on the jigsaw. Then he gave her a knife and she began to carve off sliver after sliver of wood.

All week she worked, alone, getting help from Jorge only when she was stuck. Sometimes José wandered in to watch. Lupe still mostly ignored him. But Ivette never appeared. What had happened to her? Why hadn't she come again? Lupe was too embarrassed to ask anybody, but she couldn't stop herself from thinking.

She doesn't want to see me anymore. She was just being kind to a cripple. When will I learn not to keep hoping?

I have to stop hoping.

Stop.

Hoping.

Be strong.

Alone.

It didn't occur to Lupe that she was far from alone. Jorge was helping her with the carving; she was living at the center where everybody was helping her stay alive; and she was making a present for her father. Still, she felt totally alone.

Lupe carved and sanded and tried to ignore Ivette's absence.

On Friday she felt some rumble of excitement in the air, as though the sun had more sparkle, or flowers were about to pop out of dry earth. Everyone seemed to be washing clothes. People were shining their boots and humming.

She heard Dolores talking with Rosario.

"They're coming all the way from Mazatlán? How many hours by bus?"

"About five. But my family always comes to see me once a month."

"Our family's coming this Sunday, too. My mom misses us a lot."

So that's what was happening! Families were coming to visit! Oh, she missed her family so much! Lupe felt her throat get tight. She wheeled herself off to the toy shed. Only Jorge and one boy were there. No Ivette. Lupe took the little wooden figure she'd been making all week out of its cubbyhole and sanded it.

Why hasn't Ivette come back?

She turned the figure all around, upside down, inspecting every detail. Done.

She wheeled over to the cans of paint, opened the can of black, and began to paint.

On Saturday morning the center was full of visitors, mostly parents who brought their children to be diagnosed. The parents learned how to help their children become as capable as possible. María and Consuela sat in their wheelchairs, examining each child and talking with

73

parents. By evening most of the visitors had left. But the center was far from empty. Young men and women from the village were starting to come in now.

Of course! Saturday night was party time!

When Lupe got to her room, she found several young men—strangers—lounging in front of the door. Inside, her roommates were playing cards and laughing. The men cracked jokes and laughed. The women pretended to ignore them, but sometimes they giggled and threw them sidelong glances. Lupe herself couldn't understand most of the jokes, and she thought the rest were really stupid. But it was also sort of exciting to be part of whatever was going on with these adults.

"Juan!" Rosario yelled. "We're dying of thirst! Here's some money. Go buy some sodas—six orange and three colas."

Juan clutched the money in his big fist, barged through the men, and faded away into the darkness. More people came and stood around, watching the card game, making comments. They started betting and handing around cigarettes. The room filled up with smoke and people and noise. A couple of strangers sat on Lupe's gurney, squashing against her, blocking her view. Juan lumbered back into the crowded room. Somebody handed Lupe candy and a soda. She sucked on them both, pushed people out of the way, and watched.

"It's too hot in here!" Rosario threw down her cards and pushed her way outside. Others followed, so trails of cool, clear air swirled through the smoky room. Lupe wheeled after them.

The sky outside was black. What had happened to dinner? People turned up their radios and began to dance in the courtyard, in wheelchairs, on crutches, on legs. Bottles of beer were brought in and passed around. People started laughing louder. Their eyes were shining, and their faces were glistening with sweat. A sweet smoky smell filtered through the air. A man in a black vest with silver studs all over it pushed Lupe's gurney back and forth and twirled her around. When he laughed, he threw his head back, and Lupe could see silver fillings in the back of his mouth. Everything started spinning.

The bare lightbulbs glared in her eyes. The music blared right through her. She started feeling sick, wanted to throw up, but she was scared it would go all over everybody. She wheeled back inside and covered her head with a pillow, but the world kept spinning. People screeched with laughter. Outside on the street, just beside the window, men were yelling. Bottles smashed on the stones. Somebody screamed.

Lupe pressed her face into the mattress. She was frightened. She hated this place. She wanted to go *home*!

CHAPTER THIRTEEN

Everything was quiet. A hand was stroking Lupe's hair. She opened her eyes.

Daylight. Her mother sat in front of her, smiling. Still half asleep, Lupe lifted her hand and touched her mother's cheek. It was wet. For a long, long time, all Lupe could do was stare at her mother and touch her face.

She heard somebody whispering and looked over at the doorway. Her father and Luís looked back at her. Now she saw Flor's foot poking out of her mother's shawl. Her whole family *had* come!

"You came," she said. She wanted to say more. She wanted the words to pour from her like a river, to tell them how glad she was to see them, how much she loved them and how much she wanted to go home. But all she said was "You came back."

Her mom smiled, and nodded, and wiped away her

tears. Lupe started crying, too, and her mom blotted her wet face with her shawl. Her dad gave her mom his handkerchief. Lupe and Estela both blew their noses and wiped away their tears, and everybody started laughing.

Lupe's head felt like it was full of sawdust, and her stomach felt pretty bad, too. Her three roommates were still fast asleep, even though it was ten o'clock. She quietly wheeled out into the courtyard, where a few people were sweeping up, and stopped next to some chairs. Her family arranged themselves under the trees, and they all ate oranges and cold tortillas. Then "Come," Lupe said to them. "Come."

There was nobody inside the toy shop. In the light that filtered in from the open door and windows, Lupe showed them the wood, the paints, the saws, the finished toys.

"I made something for you, Papa." She wheeled to the cubby, pulled out the small figure, and put it in her father's hand. Everyone looked down.

A wooden horse, painted black, pranced on his palm.

"That's until we get him back again," she said. Her father looked at the horse in his hand, then at Lupe. He stood there looking down at her, shaking his head.

"Do you like it, Papa?" she asked.

Her father turned the horse around in his fingers and examined it. He examined it for a long time—its legs with even the hooves carved, the ears that were way too big, the mane Lupe had had the hardest time with, and the curving tail. He took out his handkerchief and blew his nose. Finally he nodded. "Fine work, Lupe. Yes." He reached over to caress her head.

SQUEAK, SQUEAK, SQUEAK, SQUEAK, SQUEAK!

"Lupe's family!" José called out. "Did you know Lupe saved me? I fell off the cliff, and she saved me! She yelled so loud, everybody came!"

José pushed himself into the toy shop and right up to them. He lifted up his shirt and showed off his bruises. He led them outside to the cactus hedge and the cliff.

"Right here!" he said. "I fell off right here, and she saved me!"

Lupe's family heard the story from José, then a different version from Lupe, and then other versions from everybody they met.

As the day went by, more and more families filtered into the courtyard. Estela noticed that José remained alone.

"José," she said. "We brought a big feast, and there's too much for just ourselves. Can you help us out?" So Lupe was followed by her squeaking shadow once again. Today she didn't mind.

When they got to the playground, Luís climbed onto one of the rocking horses. Lupe tried to wheel right on by.

"Wait, Lupe," her mom said. "Why don't you try the swings?"

Lupe looked at the swings. She started to go toward them, then looked at José. "Let José go first," she said.

So her father lifted José into a swing and pushed him until his golden curls flew back from his forehead and his whole face shone like a little sun. He lifted Lupe into the other swing, then pushed. She sailed up. She felt the breeze against her face, felt the rope in her hands, felt her stomach rise and fall as the swing rose and fell through the air. Her mom clapped. Flor kicked his feet and gurgled

79

and cooed and hooted. Luís looked over at his sister. "Hey, Lupe, you're flying!" he called. "I'm riding a horse and you're flying!"

Flying. For just a second, Lupe felt like she really was.

Later in the afternoon, Jorge and Consuela treated Lupe's pressure sore. They asked her family to come into the room and watch. They described how sores form, and they showed them how to keep changing Lupe's position so she wouldn't get sores again at home. Home! She would be going home!

"That won't be for many weeks," Consuela said. "You still have lots of healing to do, and a whole lot to learn. And soon it'll be time for you to start school."

School?

"Well, Lupe," her father said, "if you'll be going to school here, we should go look at it, no?" They pushed her out through the squeaky gates so that they could all see the school.

The village was a lot like their own, with the same side streets of dirt and stones, impossible for gurneys or wheel-chairs. But here, a cement sidewalk led from the center up to the wide, flat, tree-lined main street. People in wheel-chairs could come and go whenever they wanted.

In the doors of the shops, women sat and talked with neighbors and knitted. Men sat in the shade under the trees, watching their children and grandchildren playing. Nobody paid any attention when people rode by on wheelchairs or gurneys. In this village, it was normal.

When Lupe's family reached the school, they stood and looked at the ramp going up the school stairs.

"Well," her father said, "I guess we'll have to build a ramp at our school, too, so Lupe can roll right inside. How would you like to help me, Luís?"

Luís's eyes lit up. "Papa, can I learn to make horses and puzzles, too, when we come back in two weeks?"

"I can show you how," Lupe said.

For just a moment, a moment so short it almost wasn't noticeable, nobody said anything. Then Luís, her dad, and her mom all spoke at once.

"Okay," Luís said.

"She does know how to run that saw," said her father.

"You've learned a lot in two weeks, Lupe," her mother joined in.

What everybody felt, but nobody said, was that even though Lupe was lying on a gurney, she was learning things she couldn't learn at home.

Hours later, Lupe lay behind the gate and watched her family walk up the sidewalk and turn the corner to take the bus back home. Gone. Had they really been there? Lupe gazed at the sidewalk, the street, the walls. The twilight turned everything to shades of gray.

Cigarette smoke drifted in the air. Lupe knew Jesús was sitting behind her, by the store. Jesús had been shot in a fight over drugs and was completely paralyzed except for one arm, with which he ran the center's small store and smoked. A bitter man with a sarcastic tongue, Jesús knew the worst gossip about everybody, or else he invented it. Lupe knew no one had come to visit him today.

She heard a rumbling noise behind her and then Adrián

and Ramón talking. She turned around to look. The two
men greeted Jesús, lifted him from his wheelchair, and
began to strap him onto a long board.

"Why are you doing that?" Lupe asked.

"It's so my leg muscles will stretch out, Lupita," Jesús
answered. "Otherwise, they'd shrivel up like a little frog
with all its blood sucked out by a fat, juicy leech." He
coughed out a laugh, lit a new cigarette, and sucked way
in. The red glow moved toward his mouth.

"Soon they'll stretch you out here too, Lupita," he said,
"like a butterfly pinned to a board. You'll try to flap your
wings, but they'll be pinned flat."

Lupe caught her breath. Could he be right? Would she
become as paralyzed as Jesús? Adrián and Ramón were

busy tightening the straps around the board. They ignored Jesús and tilted the board up so he was almost standing.

"Now your family's gone, we can strap you in and tickle you under your chinny-chin-chin. You'll yell even louder than you did for José, but you'll be trapped, TRAAAAAPPED." Jesús cackled so much he started to cough.

Lupe backed slowly away. Why weren't Adrián and Ramón saying anything?

All of a sudden Lupe noticed it was too dark, too quiet. The street in front of the center was empty. She was alone. Even if she yelled, who would help her? She backed farther away.

The end of the gurney bumped against the wall—and jolted Lupe back to herself.

Tigrilla! I am a tiger!

She wheeled the gurney straight up to Jesús and dug her fingernails into his face.

"I'll scratch you worse than that if you ever try!" she said.

Jesús burst out laughing. Lupe got his rotten cigarette breath full in the face. She wrinkled her nose in disgust and wheeled herself backward. Jesús kept laughing and coughing. Adrián and Ramón started laughing, too.

"Laugh all you want!" Lupe yelled. "I hope he coughs and coughs and COUGHS and keeps you awake all night!"

CHAPTER FOURTEEN

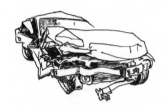

Lupe spun the gurney around and wheeled to her room as fast as she could go. None of her roommates was there. She rolled to her corner and burst into tears.

Lupe cried until the pillow was wet and she had no more strength to cry. She lay inspecting the very familiar cracks and ridges and smudges of the green wall and began picking off the paint. She smelled chicken. Her stomach growled. The sounds of everybody eating supper on the other side of the courtyard floated in the door: dishes clinking, people's voices, low music.

She heard a quiet scraping noise next to her. *Oh, no! José. Not now!*

Perfume?

She turned her head around.

María.

"It's good to cry, isn't it, Lupita?" María said gently. "I used to cry every day, every day. For two years there wasn't a day when I didn't cry. And I hated the world and everybody in it, too, day after day after day. I was nothing but a useless cripple, when all my life I'd been so gay, so outgoing and active. And life had been so much *fun*!

"You know how I came here? I was working at a flower shop, and I was engaged, with a big diamond ring on my finger. I loved to dance. I loved my fiancé. One night he got drunk at a party. I told him I would drive home this time, and I asked him to give me the keys. But no, *he* had to do it. He was the *man*. He drove like a crazy man. Actually, he drove like a drunk. We crashed, and I couldn't walk, and he left me. I lost my job, my friends. So then I cried and wished I were dead. Two whole years."

María looked at the sheet over Lupe's legs and then down at her hands as they smoothed the skirt over her own legs. As she raised her eyes to Lupe again, her voice became quieter, stronger. "Then, you know what? When I came to the center, I found that everybody here had felt the same way. They had all hated the world. Life isn't fair. We got a raw deal. Some people here were born the way they are. Some got sick. Some had accidents or got shot over drugs. But at some point they had all wanted to die, just like I did."

Lupe stared at her. "You wanted to die, too? Then why are you always smiling?"

María laughed. "Because I'm happy now," she said. "Now I feel that my life is a fight, and every day is more precious than the day before. I used to think my accident was a tragedy. Now I think it was a gift."

"A gift?" Lupe asked. "You think losing your legs was a gift?"

"Sounds crazy, doesn't it?" María agreed. "I don't know how to explain it. Maybe it's just this: I understand sorrow. I understand sorrow very well. I choose joy.

"We each have to do it alone—make that choice, I mean. But some of us are more alone than others. Jesús and José, for example, don't have families to back them up."

Lupe felt her face flush. José didn't have a family? Nobody? Jesús, too?

María went on. "Bad times can ruin us, Lupe. We can turn bitter and angry and full of hate. Bad times can also make us strong. I'm a very capable woman now. My knowledge helps people, every day. Everybody here has overcome horrible pain and hardships—much worse than mine or yours. I admire them. I love them. Even Jesús."

Lupe wondered how anybody could love Jesús, or even like him.

María noticed Lupe's look of utter disbelief.

"I'll tell you a story about Jesús, Lupe. There was a little boy who came here whose muscles were so weak he couldn't walk. He was so scared of everybody that all he could do was cling to his mama and whine. Well, that little boy needed massages, very gentle massages, for a couple of hours every day. And you know who gave him those massages, and who played with him and invented games for him that helped him get strong?"

Lupe shook her head. "Jesús?"

María nodded. "Jesús."

"Then why is he so mean? Why did he tease me? Why does he always tease Juan?"

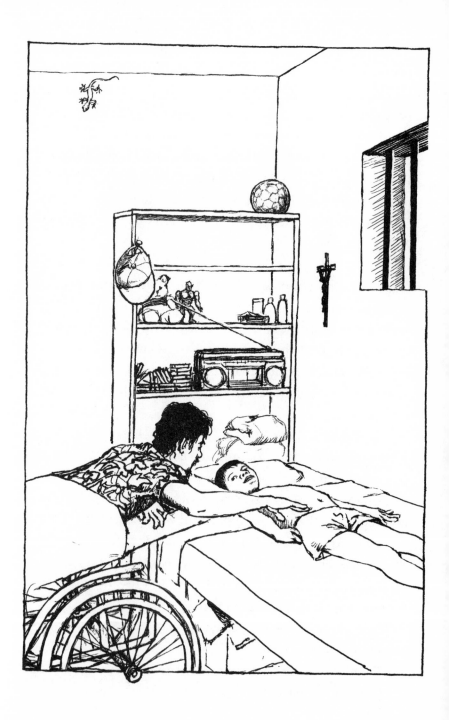

María shrugged her shoulders. "I don't know. Maybe because he's had a real hard life. Maybe because he's a human being. Why do people here get drunk and have wild, crazy parties when they know the village can kick us out because of them? Why do people take drugs even when they see the results all around them? People are getting scared to bring their children up here because of all this craziness. We make rules, everybody agrees to the rules, and then we break them. Why?"

María looked down and rubbed at a spot on her skirt. She looked back at Lupe.

"Are you perfect, Lupe?"

Lupe scowled.

Of course I'm not perfect.

I'm a cripple! I broke my back!

I fell out of a tree!

And I'm only eleven years old.

And that was a wild, crazy party, and it scared me a lot.

And Jesús is a nasty, horrible man, and Adrián and Ramón didn't help me at all. They laughed!

"Anyway," she said, "even if I ever did want to help anybody here, there's no way I could, lying on this gurney all day."

María raised her eyebrows. "You can do all sorts of things to help out, you know. You could get a broom and sweep the courtyard, for example. There's still broken glass and trash all over."

"Sweep?" Lupe asked. "That's not helping anybody. It's boring. And they should clean up their own mess."

"This is a place where the messes and the food and the

jobs belong to everybody, Lupe. Now, I'll sweep, and you hold the dustpan. If you want more 'interesting' jobs, go learn how to do them. Every person here can teach you something."

As she lay in her room that night, Lupe thought about what María had said. The only thing Lupe knew about—besides sawing a crooked line—was pressure sores. She'd seen more pressure sores treated than she could count. Many of the people who came here arrived with pressure sores, and she had watched many undergo treatment. She didn't know why she did it, because it sure wasn't something she had ever wanted to know.

CHAPTER FIFTEEN

The next morning, Lupe decided she'd had enough of toys for a while. Maybe she could check out what was going on in the metal shop.

As she rolled up the ramp and inside, Efraín sat making a wheelchair from metal rods and bicycle wheels, welding two pieces together with a blowtorch. Efraín's legs were paralyzed from polio when he was a child. Now people came from all over the world to learn from him how to make their own wheelchairs, with whatever materials they had around. Efraín learned from *them* how to keep adapting and improving his chairs.

Lupe watched a shower of white sparks spill down like water as he welded the pieces together. When he saw her watching, Efraín stopped and lifted up his visor.

"Don't watch these sparks without dark glasses, Lupe. They'll blind you, and that won't help you at all."

"Did you make my gurney?" she asked.

"Yep," he said. "We make most everything here. Different people need different chairs, because everyone's body is different, so it's easier for us to make it all. It's cheaper, it fits the person better, and it makes money for the program. Want to help?"

Help make wheelchairs? Learn to weld? Lupe stared at Efraín. Puzzles, yes. Wheelchairs, no. She backed away and rolled outside.

Consuela and Ramón were sitting in the sun. Lupe had never seen anybody with hair as orange as Consuela's. It was always rippling around because Consuela was always talking and moving. Her hair looked like flames flowing around her head. The sun glinted on Ramón's scissors as he cut a long white cloth.

"Come on over," Ramón called out. Lupe went.

Ramón got right down to business. "Time to work, Lupe. You know how you get your bedsore cleaned every day? Well, every day somebody has to cut piles and piles of those little squares from these long strips. Help Consuela wrap them in paper towels now. We'll steam them in the pressure cooker in the kitchen along with the scissors and plastic gloves. They have to be sterile when we clean you up, or you'll get infected again."

They made Lupe go wash her hands first. Then she wrapped and folded, wrapped and folded. It felt good to be in the sun, doing something helpful with other people.

Lupe kept sneaking glances at Ramón to see if she could figure out what was wrong with him. She thought she was being very subtle about it, but apparently Ramón was unusually observant.

"Looking for something?" he asked.

Lupe studied her paper towel with great attention. "Are you crippled?" she finally asked. Ramón burst out laughing.

"Not yet. Except Consuela says I'm crippled in the head. Right now I'm one of the 'temporarily' able-bodied, like you were a month ago. I'm just here hanging out with Consuela. I like it here."

Like it here? Ramón really was crippled in the head. Lupe would rather be home. If only Ivette would come back.

Juan walked by in front of them, pushing Gustavo.

"We're going for walk!" Juan announced.

Consuela smiled at Gustavo. "That Juan of yours is a good chauffeur!" she said.

Juan's face lit up with pride. Lupe thought it looked like a big red lightbulb as he pushed his friend out the gate. She lay and cut pads with Ramón and Consuela until lunchtime.

Late in the afternoon, Lupe was out on the veranda, listening to people in the kitchen talk about last Saturday night, when Consuela rolled up. "Have you seen Juan and Gustavo?" she asked.

No, Lupe hadn't. Nobody else had, either. A boy ran into the village to ask there. In a few minutes he ran back.

"People said they saw them going to the river!"

The river!

"Adrián! Ramón! Dolores!" Consuela called. "Anybody who can walk to the river!"

People sped into the courtyard from all directions. Consuela explained what had happened. Everybody started talking at once.

"Juan couldn't push Gustavo all the way down there. It's too far! Too steep!"

"All those rocks and boulders are in the way. Gustavo would fall out and smash his head on the rocks!"

"How many of us can go down there?"

Adrián, Ramón, and Martín's two sisters nodded at one another.

"Do we need to take bandages?"

"No! If anything happened, we can take care of it when you get back!"

"How about a stretcher?"

Dolores ran for a stretcher.

The group had just started for the gate when they heard a commotion outside. A procession was making its way down the sidewalk to the center.

SKREEEEEK!

The gate opened wide. One of the richest landowners in the village proceeded through. His dark brown horse was sleek and shiny, and powerful as they come. The man himself was small but strong. He sat very straight in a saddle tooled with fancy curlicues. One hand held a pommel of pure silver. A gang of children followed him in, laughing and pointing up and calling, "Gustavo! Gustavo!"

High up in the saddle, his arms tied tight around the landowner's middle so he wouldn't fall off, rode Gustavo. He was sopping wet and had a big orange-soda mustache. Almost lost in the crowd of children came Juan, pushing the empty wheelchair. He was just as wet as Gustavo, and his teeth were orange inside his grinning orange mouth.

The landowner stopped his horse and untied Gustavo.

Several people helped him slide down into his wheelchair. The landowner sat erect in the saddle and waited. Everyone got quiet so that they could hear him. This was a man who was used to having people get quiet when he spoke.

"Good evening, neighbors," he said. "When I rode out, I saw that young man carrying the other one down toward the river. I watched him carry the chair sometimes while his friend crawled over the rocks. When I came back, I saw they'd been swimming. They looked tired. It's a long way back up the hill. Not hard for a horse."

He touched the brim of his hat, turned, and rode slowly up the sidewalk. The back of his shirt was wet with river water and orange soda.

CHAPTER SIXTEEN

Lupe had been at the center for more than three weeks, and was getting used to life there. Lunch was over, and most people were in their rooms having a siesta. Lupe rolled over to the gate. The little store was closed. Jesús was taking his siesta, too. Lupe could lie there alone, look up the road, and feel sad in perfect peace and quiet. She was dozing, feeling comfortably sad and lonely, when the clopping of hooves on the loose stones in the road woke her up.

A young man rode up to the gate on a donkey. Lupe recognized him as Consuela's brother who came down from the mountains to visit her. He dismounted, tied the reins to the gate, opened it—SKREEK—and walked into the courtyard. Lupe rested her chin on her hands and looked the donkey over.

She couldn't help thinking about El Diablo—his smooth, shiny black coat, his powerful muscles, his saddle oiled to perfection. He really was much finer than that rich man's horse Gustavo had ridden.

But this donkey was pitiful. His dull gray hair stood out in all directions. His saddle was scuffed and cracked. His great big head hung down.

"You sure aren't El Diablo," Lupe said to him. "You look like a four-legged old sweater full of moth holes."

She reached up to stroke the donkey's muzzle. The donkey jerked back. Lupe left her hand on the grille of the gate. She talked. She sang the songs she used to sing for El Diablo. The donkey rubbed his nose against her hand.

Lupe stroked his fuzzy forehead and his neck. She noticed something dark on his leg and pulled the reins. The donkey walked a step closer. High on his leg near his chest was a big sore, probably a wound from a fight with another donkey, or a horse. The sore was infected and red. Flies crawled on it. They buzzed around Lupe's hand as she pushed the hair back from the sore and inspected it.

All at once she whirled the gurney around and rolled to the clinic where the supplies were kept. No one was around. She took down a paper towel–wrapped pair of plastic gloves from the low shelf and pulled out the bottle of soap and one bottle of boiled water, a roll of adhesive tape, and the jar of sugar-honey. Now, where were the packets of gauze?

They were on the top shelf of the cupboard. The shelves were too high up for her to reach.

Just like María.

I can't reach up high.

Lupe heard a rolling squeak behind her. *Blessed sound! José!*

"José, see where they keep the packets of gauze up there?" she asked.

The boy looked up at the high shelf.

"Can you get me some?"

José climbed from his walker onto the table, then crawled across Lupe's gurney to the cupboard. He opened it, pulled himself up, and reached as high as he could. Two inches too short.

Lupe shoved her pillow in front of her and folded it in half. José stood on the pillow and grabbed. A handful of packets fell onto the gurney. He knelt down next to Lupe and helped gather all the supplies close to her, blocking them with the pillow so they wouldn't fall off. Lupe spun her gurney around, and they rode back to the donkey.

Carefully she pulled on the gloves as she had seen the others do and unwrapped one of the gauze pads. José poured soap onto the pad. Lupe picked up the reins with her left hand and pulled the donkey close. With her right hand, she washed all around the sore, swabbing the pus and dirt away. The donkey trembled and tried to back away. Lupe held tight to the reins and soothed him, talking as she worked. The donkey stood quietly. His nostrils widened only when she rubbed too hard.

José poured water onto new pads. Lupe washed off the soap, then dried the wound with more pads. Wet pads littered the ground.

Lupe pulled the jar of sugar-honey from under the pillow and tried to twist the lid off. It refused to move. Lupe handed it to José, but he couldn't open it either. The lid was too big for their hands, and it was glued shut with sugar-honey. She had José hold it while she tried to twist the top with both hands. Her hair stuck to the pot. The top didn't budge. She tried to pry it off with her teeth. Sweet stickiness trickled into her mouth and plastered her cheeks and chin. She started to sweat and curse under her breath.

"Need some help, doctors?"

Adrián stood next to her gurney, his arms held out to her from his crutches. Lupe's heart sank. Now he would take over, or he would laugh and tease her. She gave him the plastic container. Adrián twisted open the lid and returned it to her, then stood waiting. Was he letting her do it?

Lupe hesitated, then spooned out some sugar-honey, wiped it onto a white square of gauze that José held, and pushed it against the donkey's sore. Uh-oh. She couldn't hold the bandage and cut the tape at the same time. She looked up at Adrián. He gave the tape to José, who held it for him to cut, then taped it across the pad and onto the donkey's hair.

"Next time," Adrián said, "we'd better shave off some hair first."

Next time?

She scooped another glob of sugar-honey onto a pad and watched as they pressed it on, covered it with another pad, and taped it all down. The three surveyed their work. Lupe grinned, first at Adrián, then at José. Adrián shook hands with them both. Lupe heard a noise behind them. She turned. Everyone in the courtyard was clapping.

"Good job, Doctora Lupita, Doctor José!"

"Hey, Lupe!" Jesús called out. "If I ever get pressure sores again, I'll come to you!"

Lupe blushed as she took off her gloves and dropped them on the ground.

"Not so fast, Doctora Tigra." María carried a broom and dustpan across the arms of her wheelchair. "Those gloves are expensive. You know perfectly well we have to wash and sterilize them so we can use them again. Remember how you told me that people should sweep up their own messes? Well, look at the ground. Those pads full of pus and soap and donkey blood aren't flower petals. I'll hold the dustpan."

As María held the dustpan, Lupe swept, keeping her eyes on the ground so no one could see how proud she was.

When they were finished, María took the broom and the full dustpan in her left hand. With her right she shook Lupe's hand.

"Welcome, *compañera*," she said quietly. "And come to the clinic tomorrow morning at seven. A new patient is coming. I want you to meet her."

María turned and wheeled off across the courtyard.

CHAPTER SEVENTEEN

Lupe lay on her gurney in the examination room, behind María and Efraín. Lupe remembered what María had said about her gift. María and Efraín would be able to help a lot of the children who had come today, just as they'd helped her. She could see the line of visitors outside, parents sitting with their children on the pink and green painted benches, one boy rocking on a purple swing. Everybody was quiet, basking in the warm morning sun. Inside, the cold still slept in the thick adobe walls, and Lupe rubbed her arms hard, trying to get her blood moving.

A silhouette blocked the doorway, moved into the room, and turned into a woman with a bundle of blankets in her arms. Out of the bundle rose a mass of tangled black hair surrounding a little face with two round, fearful black eyes. Gently María took the bundle and unwrapped the blankets to examine the child.

For almost a month Lupe had been living at the center with people who had all kinds of disabilities, but she wasn't prepared for Jesica.

Jesica was skin and bones. Her frail arms hugged herself tight. One leg was shriveled, the other swollen. Both feet bent way in. The swollen foot had a deep, infected sore on top, where she had tried to walk on it. María turned the little girl over. Sores covered her bottom.

Jesica's mother was so embarrassed that she began to speak very quickly, but so softly they could hardly hear her. "Jesica has little feeling from the waist down. She doesn't know when she poops or pees. She looks like a baby, but she is almost five years old. I work all day to feed my children. They are alone too much."

María nodded. "I understand." She handed the little girl back to her mother.

"What happened?" she asked.

"Three days after she was born," her mother said, "the doctor gave her an injection—here, where her bottom has no fat now. That's where he stuck in the needle. It got infected, with a big boil. Soon Jesica didn't move her legs anymore."

"Why did she need an injection?" Efraín asked.

"The doctor didn't say."

María and Efraín looked at each other. They had seen other cases like this.

"Well," Efraín said. "She still has some feeling in her legs and can probably learn to walk. We'll start on those pressure sores and on a cast to straighten her legs. Then we'll help her learn to take care of herself. How long can you stay?"

The woman looked down. "I have to leave tonight. The other children . . . it is difficult. And I have no money—nothing."

"We never turn people away because they can't pay," María told her. "Jesica can stay here while she gets well. A family in the village looks after children sometimes. I'm sure they'll take Jesica. And we have someone here who will help her during the day."

She looked at Lupe. "Okay?"

At first Lupe didn't understand. When she did, she was so stunned she couldn't speak.

"Me? Oh. Uh, yes. Yes!"

Efraín laughed. "Go outside and wait, then. We'll get somebody to bring the family here for Jesica. We still have a long line of people to see."

Lupe followed Jesica and her mother outside, past the waiting, hopeful faces, and into the courtyard.

"Do you want to swing?" she asked Jesica. The child searched Lupe's face, then nodded with great solemnity. Her mother put her into a swing. Lupe held her gurney in front of the swing and pushed, very slightly. Jesica swung back and forth, staring, staring. Ten or fifteen minutes went by. Lupe pushed, Jesica swung and stared.

"Gift," thought Lupe. "Treating a little girl's pressure sores and teaching her how to poop and pee when she wants. It's not a gift I'd ever choose. I'd much rather have my legs back, and El Diablo, everything we lost. I'd rather be home. But I'm not home. I'm here. And today—"

"Lupe! Lupe!" a girl's voice called.

Lupe turned. Ivette was walking toward her, waving, holding hands with a woman wearing a flowery dress and big blue earrings. Ivette! Lupe wanted to come over and hug her. But at the same time she wanted to run away. Why hadn't Ivette come before this? Maybe she didn't really like Lupe and had come to see somebody else. But Ivette was already next to her.

"Mama, this is my friend Lupe. Lupe, Mama. Lupe, I got a bad cold right after I met you, and then we had to go visit my cousins. I couldn't come until now. We're going to take care of a little girl named Jesica. Do you know who she is?"

Lupe smiled at Jesica and her mother. "A girl named Jesica? Oh, I sure do!"

They all gave Jesica a bath in the outdoor sink. They shampooed her hair and washed her skinny little body. Jesica babbled and splashed, and she babbled on as they dried her off and dressed her in clean clothes.

Later, in the treatment room, Jorge guided Lupe as she scrubbed out Jesica's sores and filled them with sugar-honey. Lupe thought they were gross and scary. But she knew she had had the very same kind of sore herself, and now she was almost well. She cleaned them thoroughly, so that Jesica could get well, too.

Jesica's mother, Ivette, and Ivette's mother all watched. One thing was clear to everybody: Lupe was good at this.

In the afternoon, Adrián made a cast for Jesica's swollen leg. First he pulled a stocking onto her leg, then he covered it all with gucky wet gray plaster, leaving the sore on her foot uncovered so Lupe could treat it. Lupe and Ivette sat in the sunny playground playing with Jesica until her cast got white and hard as a rock. Adrián cut it off and

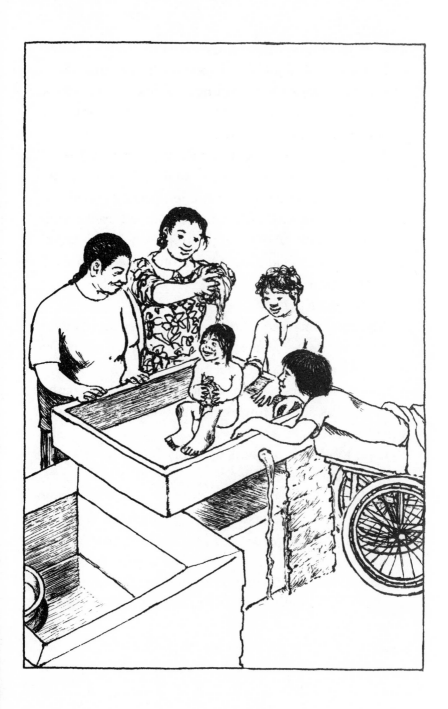

took it back to the workshop, where he began to make a mold for Jesica's leg brace. Lupe watched intently. Soon Jesica would walk on two strong legs. Jesica would walk, and maybe run and climb. To be able to help a little girl do all that—now *that* was a gift.

The sun was behind the mountains when Jesica's mother hugged and kissed her daughter good-bye, then handed her to Ivette's mother and left. Jesica sobbed. She wailed. She screamed as her mother walked up the same cement sidewalk where Lupe had seen her own family walk away. Lupe held Jesica's hand and smiled. Jesica was going to be just fine.

Ivette turned to Lupe.

"Are you coming to school soon?" she asked. "Can you come to our house? Mama, can we go to the toy shop for a while and make toys?"

"Go ahead, Ivette," her mother said. "And yes, Lupe, come visit us soon. How about as soon as you get your wheelchair?"

Lupe looked at her and suddenly found herself grinning—grinning wide, wide.

A wheelchair! In a few weeks, her pressure sores would be healed. She could get off this big old tank of a gurney and zip all over the place.

A wheelchair.

Maybe she'd ask Efraín if he'd teach her how to weld.

Maybe they could start tomorrow?

AFTERWORD

The "center" in this story is based on a real place in the village of Ajoya about eighty miles north of Mazatlán. PROJIMO, or, in English, Project of Rehabilitation Organised by Disabled Youth of Western Mexico, is an offshoot of a village primary health care program started more than thirty years ago by David Werner, an American who still lives at the project part time. The rest of the year he travels around the world in search of things he can learn from and share with other village-based health and disability programs.

I have set the story about fifteen years ago, when I first visited PROJIMO and began to get to know some of the people who lived there. All the events in the story that take place at the center are real and did happen there, though I've created some composites and have not used real names. There was one particular girl at PROJIMO whose courage and radiance served as my inspiration for Lupe. She was paralyzed from the waist down, she began her own rehabilitation when she healed the sore on a donkey waiting at the gate, and she helped in the rehabilitation of a younger girl exactly as described in the story. Everything else about Lupe and her family is entirely fictional.

PROJIMO has undergone many changes since the events I describe. The village where the center exists lies in an area of heavy traffic in opium and cocaine. Many residents of the village are much poorer than before, and a number of men and older boys have been killed because of drug wars and kidnappings. A third of the remaining population has moved elsewhere. Many people are too afraid to bring their children up to the village for consultations. PROJIMO Skills Training and Work Program continues to operate there, but most of the rehabilitation staff have moved to a second center down the mountain near the highway to Mazatlán.

Today there is a main municipal hospital in Mazatlán, which is modern, busy, and quite good. The poor are well cared for there (though they do have to cover the cost of medicine). But fifteen or twenty years ago, before this hospital existed, it was not at all uncommon for a family who went to a public hospital to be ruined financially because a family member would not be released until full payment was made.